MURPHY

TATIANA TONKS

Illustrations by

CARLOS FREIRE

Scholastic Canada Ltd.

For the Carruthers gang:
Amber, Sarah, Preston, Troy,
and Buttons the cat.
T.T.

Scholastic Canada Ltd.
123 Newkirk Road, Richmond Hill, Ontario, Canada L4C 3G5

Scholastic Inc.
730 Broadway, New York, NY 10003, USA

Ashton Scholastic Pty Limited
PO Box 579, Gosford, NSW 2250, Australia

Ashton Scholastic Limited
Private Bag 1, Penrose, Auckland, New Zealand

Scholastic Publications Ltd.
Villiers House, Clarendon Avenue, Leamington Spa
Warwickshire CV32 5PR, UK

6 5 4 3 2 1 Printed in Hong Kong 2 3 4 5 6/9

Canadian Cataloguing in Publication Data

Tonks, Tatiana
Murphy

ISBN 0-590-73759-7

I. Freire, Carlos, 1943- . II. Title

PS8589.O55M8 1992 jC813'.54 C92-094239-0

Patrick was a very good boy. He was almost like an angel. Sometimes Patrick got into trouble, but it was never his fault. Patrick had a cat named Murphy. Murphy was a terrible, horrible cat. When Patrick got into trouble, his cat was always behind it.

"Go ahead, take another piece of pie!" Murphy told him once. "Your mom will never notice!"

But Patrick's mother DID notice, and Patrick was in trouble up to his neck.

"Come on, it's only a tiny little tree," Murphy said another time. "Anybody who's not chicken can climb it!"

Well, Patrick wasn't chicken, but he couldn't climb the tree. When he fell he broke his arm and had to go to the hospital. Patrick was in trouble up to his ears.

At Christmas, Murphy told Patrick to peek at his presents.

"But that's bad!" said Patrick, who was good, like an angel.

"Tomorrow you'll find out what they all are anyway, won't you?" asked Murphy. That made perfect sense to Patrick. But later, when he tried to explain it to his father, it came out all wrong. Patrick was in trouble again — right up to his eyebrows.

One afternoon, Patrick drew a picture of a rocket ship.
When Murphy saw it, he said, "Wow! That's the most super-fantastic picture I ever saw! Why don't you surprise your mom and draw the same one on the wall with your crayons?" Patrick thought it was a great idea, but his mother didn't. Murphy got Patrick into trouble again — all the way over his head.

On Patrick's birthday, Murphy suggested he taste the cake early. But Patrick said, "Do you remember what happened last time?" and he didn't take any.

Then Murphy said, "Well, why don't you climb up on the roof and see if anyone's coming to the party yet?"

But Patrick shook his head. "Forget it! Do you want me to break my other arm?"

"Hey, I know!" said Murphy. "Why don't we see what's inside that box with the big red ribbon?"

"No thanks," said Patrick. "I think I'll just wait and let it be a surprise."

"How about a treat for your mom?" Murphy tried. "We could go to Mr. Gordon's garden and pick a big bunch of flowers for her!" But Patrick didn't want to do that either, so Murphy curled up and went to sleep.

Later, after Patrick had blown out the birthday candles and all the guests had gone home, his mother gave him a big birthday hug. "You've been so good today, Patrick," she said. "Why do you get into so much trouble sometimes?"

Patrick was glad that she had finally asked.

"It's Murphy!" he said, pointing to the cat "He makes me do all those terrible, horrible things!"

"Really?" his mother asked. "And how does he do that?"

"He tells me to!" said Patrick. "Go on, Murphy, show her how you do it!"

But Murphy just opened one eye and said, "Meow!"

"He's mad at me," Patrick explained, "because I didn't listen to him today."

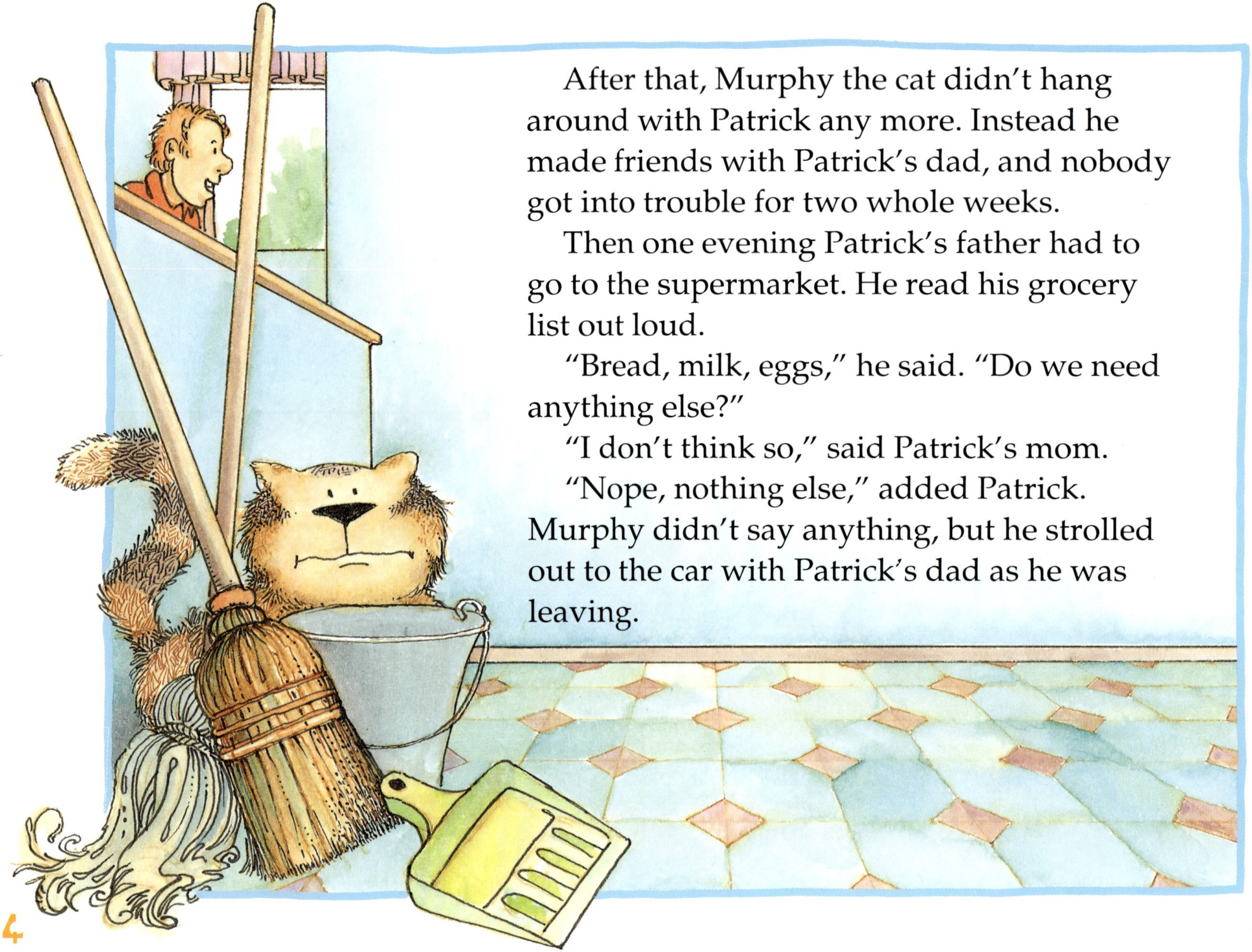

After that, Murphy the cat didn't hang around with Patrick any more. Instead he made friends with Patrick's dad, and nobody got into trouble for two whole weeks.

Then one evening Patrick's father had to go to the supermarket. He read his grocery list out loud.

"Bread, milk, eggs," he said. "Do we need anything else?"

"I don't think so," said Patrick's mom.

"Nope, nothing else," added Patrick. Murphy didn't say anything, but he strolled out to the car with Patrick's dad as he was leaving.

Patrick's father came back with two bags of groceries, but he didn't have any bread or milk or eggs. Instead he had lots of potato chips, some marshmallows and a big raw fish.

"Now what's got into your father?" wondered Patrick's mom.

"Something funny is going on," said Patrick.

The fish was too big, so Murphy helped them eat it.

That Saturday, Patrick's father decided to paint the house.
"What colour are you going to paint it?" asked Patrick.
"I'm not sure," said his dad. "Maybe grey."
"Or a nice dark brown," Patrick's mom suggested.
Murphy just said, "Meow!"

Patrick and his mom went shopping while Patrick's dad painted. When they came home, they got a big surprise. Patrick's dad had finished painting the house — bright orange, with pink and green stripes!

Patrick's dad looked a bit nervous.

"Orange?! Green and pink?!" cried Patrick's mom. "It looks horrible! What in the world made you do such a terrible thing?"

Patrick's father didn't say a word. He just looked at Murphy, and Murphy yawned and licked his paw.

"Uh oh!" thought Patrick. He took his father by the hand. "Come on, Dad," he said. "We need to have a talk!"

And you know, whatever Patrick said, it worked! Patrick's dad didn't get into any more trouble, ever again.

And what did Murphy do?
Well . . . that's another story!